Pickled Peppers

Pickled peppers

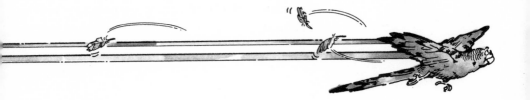

by NANCY McARTHUR

illustrated by DENISE BRUNKUS

SCHOLASTIC INC.
New York Toronto London Auckland Sydney

To Stella, Red, Donald,
Sylvia, and Lorraine Moore.

Special thanks to
Pat Jenkins, Arlene Lehtinen,
Becky Croom, and Dale Anglund.
—N. M.

For Mom and Dad
—D. B.

ISBN 0-590-40997-2

Text copyright © 1988 by Nancy McArthur
Illustrations copyright © 1988 by Denise Brunkus
All rights reserved. Published by Scholastic Inc.

Hello Reader is a registered trademark of Scholastic Inc.

12 11 10 9 8 7 6 5 4 3   8 9/8 0 1 2 3 3/9

Printed in the U.S.A.   08
First Scholastic printing, April 1988

Suzie hugged Aunt Helen's dog good-bye.

"I wish I could keep you, Puddles," she said. Pud nuzzled her with his fuzzy face.

Next month, Aunt Helen was moving to another city. Her new apartment would not allow pets.

"I wish you could keep him, too," said Aunt Helen. "But I know someone who will give him a good home, even though she already has a dog."

128986

Pud stuck his head out the car window and licked Suzie's nose.

Aunt Helen waved as she drove away. "If you change your mind," she called to Mom, "let me know!"

Suzie did not want to give up. "Please, can we keep Pud? Please, please, please?"

"No," said Mom. "We've been over this a million times."

"But why not?"

"You know why," said Dad. "Pud was here all month while Helen was on vacation. You promised to feed and walk him. Then you kept forgetting."

"And I got stuck with all the work," said Mom.

"But I promise I'll do it," said Suzie.

"You promised before," said Dad. He put his arm around her. "You're just not ready to take care of a pet."

Mom said gently, "We'll get you a dog when you're a little older."

"When you show you can take care of a pet," said Dad. "We promise."

Suzie did not want another dog later. She wanted Pud now.

Getting older would take too long.

But how could she show she could take care of a pet with no pet to take care of?

She went out to the backyard to think.

"Hi, Suzie," said Mrs. Brown next door. "Why do you look so sad?"

Suzie told her.

"I'm going away for two weeks," Mrs.
Brown said. "I need someone to take care of
my parakeet."

"Can I do it?" asked Suzie.

She liked Bitsy. The little green bird
could talk.

Mrs. Brown had taught her to say, "Peter
Piper picked a peck of pickled peppers."

If you said it to Bitsy, she said it back to you.

Suzie always got the tongue twister
tangled up, but Bitsy did it right every time.

Mrs. Brown showed Suzie how to do everything.

"What if she gets out of the cage?" asked Suzie.

"Be very careful not to let her out. But if it happens, quickly close the door of the room. Then you wait a long, long time. When she gets hungry, she'll go back in the cage."

Mrs. Brown said, "You have to give her food and water. And talk to her. And clean the cage. That part is messy."

"I can do it," said Suzie.

"And never forget?" asked Mrs. Brown.

"Never," said Suzie.

"You've got the job," said Mrs. Brown. "I'm counting on you."

Mom and Dad agreed Suzie could do it.

"If you fizzle out," said Mom, "at least I won't have to take the bird for walks."

Suzie did everything right for Bitsy the
first day. And the second day. And the third.

Suzie almost forgot a few times to clean
the cage. But she did it, even though she
didn't like to.

Her friend Annie came every day to say
the tongue twister to Bitsy.

"I have to do it because you don't say it right," Annie said.

"I do, too," said Suzie. "Peter Piper picked a peck of packled pickers."

"Pickled peppers," said Annie, "not packled pickers."

They both started to giggle.

"Only two more days," Suzie told Bitsy
while she cleaned the cage. "Then you
can go home, and I can get Pud. I can
hardly wait!"

But suddenly Bitsy hopped out of the cage
so fast Suzie could not stop her.

"Come back," said Suzie.

Bitsy hopped away.

Suzie reached for her. Bitsy flew up. All
Suzie got was a handful of air.

And she fell over the couch.

Bitsy landed on a lamp. Suzie closed the
door to keep her in the room.

She did not want to wait a long, long time.
She wanted to go out and play with Annie.

Maybe she could sneak up and catch Bitsy.

Suzie did not want Bitsy to see that she
was sneaking up.

So she tiptoed backward. But she tripped
over a footstool and bumped into the lamp.

When she tried to catch the lamp, she fell
over a chair.

The chair thumped into a table, which
knocked over another lamp.

A pile of books went flying.

So did Bitsy.

The door opened. "What's going on in here?" asked Mom.

"Close the door!" yelled Suzie.

A little green streak zoomed out of the room.

"No flying in the house!" yelled Mom. "Follow that bird!"

They looked all over the house. No Bitsy.

"I'll get her to talk," said Suzie. "Then we can hear where she is."

She said to the kitchen, "Peter Piper picked a pack of peckled pickers."

The basement door opened.

"What's going on?" asked Dad.

"Close the door!" shouted Suzie and Mom.

He did. They told him what was going on.

"I'll help," he said. "Peter Piper picked a peck of packled pippers."

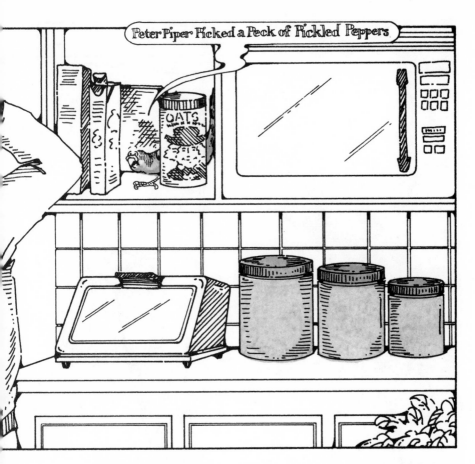

"No," said Suzie, "Peter Piper packed a pick
of pickled packers."

"Let me do it," said Mom. "Peter Piper
pecked a pick of peckled papers."

"Peckled?" said Suzie.

"Papers?" said Dad.

They all laughed.

Then a little voice said, "Peter Piper picked
a peck of pickled peppers."

Bitsy was behind the cereal boxes. Suzie
slowly sneaked up.   19

They heard a knock on the back screen door. The door opened.

"What's going on?" asked Annie.

"Close the door!" they all yelled.

Too late. Bitsy flew right out of the house.

They ran out in the yard. They all said the tongue twister to bushes and trees.

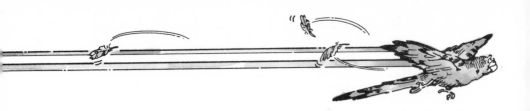

No word from Bitsy.

"We need more people," said Suzie. She and Annie ran to find more kids.

Some came running to help. Some went running to get others.

Soon you could hear "Peter Piper" all over. Front yards. Backyards. Up in trees. Under bushes.

The mailman stopped to listen when he got to Suzie's house. He heard pickled peppers everywhere. He also heard some packled pippers, peckled papers, and pickled packles.

Suzie ran out with a big bird cage.

"Here's a letter for you," the mailman said. "There's a big paw print on the back."

"This must be from my dog," said Suzie excitedly. "He's really almost my dog."

"Your dog writes letters?" asked the mailman.

"I have to find Mrs. Brown's bird first. Then he can be my real dog. Everything's going wrong today."

"What's going on?" asked the mailman.

"If you see a little green bird, let me know," said Suzie. She crawled into the bushes saying, "Peter Piper packed a pick of packled pippers."

Peter Piper Picked a Peck of Pickled Peppers!

"This must be some nutty new game," said the mailman. He decided to try it.

"Peter Piper picked a peck of pickled peppers," he said. "I was always good at tongue twisters. A peck of packled pippers Peter Packer pipped."

From a low branch overhead a little voice said, "Peter Piper picked a peck of pickled peppers."

He looked up. It was a little green bird.

"Here's your bird," he called to Suzie. "Do you want me to try to grab it?"

"No," said Suzie's voice from behind the bushes. "That just scares her away."

She crawled out and put the cage under the tree. She put some birdseed and grapes next to it.

Then she sat down on the front steps to wait a long, long time.

Annie and some others came over to wait with her.

Mom and Dad went in to make pizza for all the kids who helped.

They sat there a long, long time.

"Maybe we better get a ladder and try to catch her," said Annie.

"No, she must be tired and hungry and thirsty," said Suzie. "I hope she'll come down soon."

"What's a pickled pepper, anyway?" asked Annie.

"Maybe it's a green pepper with pickles stuck all over it," said Suzie.

"No, they'd roll off," said Annie.

Mom came out and sat down to help them wait.

"What's a pickled pepper?" Annie asked her.

"It's a green pepper that's been pickled — soaked in spices. You can pickle different things. Even watermelon. A regular pickle is really a little cucumber," Mom explained.

"Yuck," said Suzie.

Suddenly Bitsy moved. She fluttered to the ground.

She pecked at the food. She looked around for a long time. Then she hopped into the cage.

Suzie tiptoed over slowly and closed the cage door. Bitsy was safe.

"Yay!" everybody yelled.

At the pizza party Suzie read the letter from Pud.

"Dogs don't write letters," said Annie.

"My aunt wrote down what he wanted to say."

The letter said, *"I am fine. How are you? When are you coming to see me? Love, Pud."*

There was another big paw print at the bottom.

Suzie said, "I showed I can take care of a
pet. So now can I have Pud? Please, please,
please?"

Mom and Dad looked at each other.

"Yes," said Mom. "I guess I'll be glad to
see good old Pud. At least he doesn't do
tongue twisters."

"Me, too," said Dad. "I'm glad he doesn't
fly."

The pizza had pieces of green pepper
on it.

"Is this pickled pepper?" asked Annie with
a grin.

Suzie took a bite. "No, it's packled pipper,"
she said with a giggle.

After the pizza party Suzie called Aunt
Helen to tell her the good news.

Then she asked to talk to Pud.

Pud woofed over the phone. He sounded
happy.

When Mrs. Brown came to get Bitsy, Suzie told her what happened.

"It wasn't your fault she got out," said Mrs. Brown. "What counts is that you got her back safely."

"Yesterday Bitsy taught me to say the tongue twister right," said Suzie. "I kept doing it wrong. She kept doing it right. Then I got it. Listen. Peter Piper picked a peck of pickled peppers."

"Good for you," said Mrs. Brown.

Then Bitsy said, "Peter Piper pecked a pick of packled pippers."

Can you say the whole tongue twister?

Peter Piper picked a peck of pickled peppers.
A peck of pickled peppers Peter Piper picked.
If Peter Piper picked a peck of pickled peppers,
Where is the peck of pickled peppers
Peter Piper picked?